Disney Junior Early Reader Collection

LEVEL 1

Sofia is an eight-year-old girl living in Enchancia. She became a princess when her mother married the king. Sofia goes to princess school at Royal Prep with other princes and princesses, but she has friends in the village, too. She has a magical amulet that gives her the power to hear and talk to animals.

Amber is Sofia's sister and James's twin. She loves everything about being a princess, especially the tiaras, gowns, and parties. Amber gives Sofia lots of tips about how to be a proper princess, but she has a lot to learn from Sofia, too.

James is Sofia's brother and Amber's twin. When he's not busy with princely duties, James likes to be outside playing sports like soccer, flying derby, and flying horseshoes. He also has a great imagination and enjoys all kinds of games.

Roland is Sofia's father and the king of Enchancia. He fell in love with Miranda when she brought a pair of shoes she had made for him to the castle. They were married soon after. The job of being the king keeps Roland very busy, but being a father to Sofia, Amber, and James is just as important to him, and he always makes time for his family.

Miranda is Sofia's mother. When they lived in the village, Sofia helped Miranda make shoes for people at the cobbler shop. But now that she is married to the king, Miranda is queen of Enchancia and mom to Amber and James, too.

Welcome to
Royal Prep

Written by Lisa Ann Marsoli

Illustrated by Character Building Studio

and the Disney Storybook Art Team

DISNEY PRESS

Open House at Royal Prep
is almost here!
Sofia can't wait!

The fairies give everyone a job.

Sofia, Hildegard, and Khalid
clean and stack and tidy.

Jin and James decorate
from top to bottom.

Clio and Jun help bake the snacks.
Amber and Maya water and sweep.

Next the children practice
for the Open House show.
They go over their dance steps.
They read poems.

They sing and play songs.
They want the show to be perfect.

Finally, the children choose
their best artwork.
"This is Cedric, the royal
sorcerer," James says.

"Once he used magic
and turned himself into
a mushroom!"
Sofia picks a wall hanging.
Amber can't decide what to show.

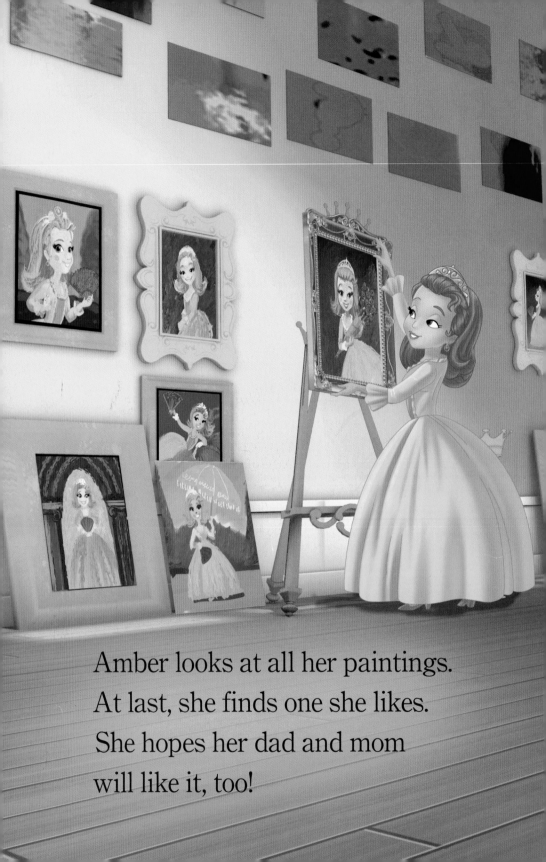

Amber looks at all her paintings.
At last, she finds one she likes.
She hopes her dad and mom
will like it, too!

After Amber leaves,
Sofia spots some jars of paint.
"Can you help me put these away?"
she asks James.

James picks up the jars.
They start to slip.
"Uh-oh!" he cries.
Paint flies everywhere!

"Amber is going to be so
mad at me!" cries James.
Sofia and James try to
wipe away the paint.

They make the mess worse!
The painting is ruined!
"We can't tell Amber," says James.

"I'm going to switch the paintings,"
James says.
"It won't work," says Sofia.
"Amber picked that painting
just for Mom and Dad."

James finds a blank canvas.
He copies the painting he ruined.
It looks terrible!

James still wants to fix his mistake.
He opens the windows wide.

"I'll say the wind blew the painting over!" he says. "Why don't you just tell the truth?" asks Sofia.

"Tell the truth about what?"
asks Amber.
She looks at Sofia and James.
She sees her ruined painting!

"I'm sorry," James says.
"It was an accident."
"What will I show Mom and Dad at
Open House?" cries Amber.
"That was my best painting."

Later, Sofia has an idea.

She shares it with Amber.

"Do you think our parents

will like it?" Amber asks.

"They will love it!" Sofia says.

Amber goes to work.
She stays out of sight.
She wants to surprise King Roland
and Queen Miranda.

Sofia and James help Amber
with the painting.

At last, it is finished!

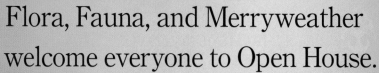

Flora, Fauna, and Merryweather
welcome everyone to Open House.

Then the children put on their show.

Next it's time to visit each class.
King Roland sees James's statue.
"Look, it's Cedric!" says the king.
"I'd know him anywhere!"

The king and queen
admire Sofia's wall hanging.

Finally, it's time to see
Amber's painting. Her parents love it!
"It's our first family portrait!"
exclaims the queen.

The king and queen
hang the painting in a special place.
Everyone agrees it is
Amber's best yet—even Amber!

Princess Lesson

A true princess
always tells the truth.

Jake is the leader of the Never Land pirate crew. He loves being a pirate and is always ready for adventure and action! Jake is never without his trusty sword, and he's great at spotting treasure through his spyglass. With the help of his mateys, there is no pirate problem he can't solve!

Izzy is a team player who always knows the right thing to do. Izzy's prized pirate possession is her pouch of Pixie Dust. Her Never Land fairy friends gave it to her so that she and her friends can fly—but only in emergencies!

Cubby has a keen sense of direction and is a master at following and drawing maps. Cubby is a cautious pirate and sometimes his nerves get the better of him. But when the going gets tough, Cubby always manages to summon his courage and overcome his fears.

Skully is the official lookout for Jake's crew. He keeps a weather eye on the horizon for trouble and treasure alike. On every adventure, Skully is always ready with an encouraging "Crackers!" or funny joke.

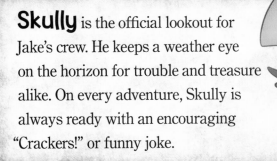

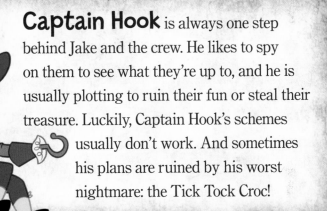

Captain Hook is always one step behind Jake and the crew. He likes to spy on them to see what they're up to, and he is usually plotting to ruin their fun or steal their treasure. Luckily, Captain Hook's schemes usually don't work. And sometimes his plans are ruined by his worst nightmare: the Tick Tock Croc!

Mr. Smee is Captain Hook's loyal first mate. He is always at Hook's side ready to help out on a treasure hunt. But when things don't go as planned, Smee knows that he can count on Jake and the crew to help him and Hook out of a tight spot.

Ahoy, mateys! Do you want to join my pirate crew? Then just say the pirate password: "Yo-ho-ho!" As part of my crew, you'll need to learn the Never Land pirate pledge.

TODAY'S PIRATE PLEDGE

A good pirate doesn't take his matey's treasure.

Surfin' Turf

Written by Melinda LaRose

Based on the episode written by Nicole Dubuc

Illustrated by Character Building Studio

and the Disney Storybook Art Team

D𝒾SNEY PRESS

Marina the mermaid is teaching
Jake and his crew how to surf.

"Yoo-hoo!" calls a new mermaid.
"What a fun surfy-thing. Can I try?"

Who does the mermaid look like?

"That's not a mermaid," says Izzy.
"It's Hook!"
"Look alive, mateys!" yells Skully.
"I see the fin of a sea monster!"

"It's not a monster," says Izzy.
"It's Smee!"
"Now I've got the surfy-thing,"
says Hook. "Let's go!"

How many flowers
do you see on the
surfboard?

"Those footprints are from Smee's fins," says Jake. "It looks like Hook is heading for Red River," says Cubby.

Can you find Red River on the map?

"Careful, Cap'n," says Smee.
"Don't wake the Tick Tock Croc."

Hook bumps the Croc
with the surfboard.
The Croc begins to chase them!
Hook and Smee jump into the river.

"Hook is getting away," says Marina. "They're heading for Rainbow River," says Cubby.

Can you find the Tick Tock Croc?

"Hook is way ahead of us!" says Skully.
"Too bad you aren't mermaids.
Then you could swim down the river,"
says Marina.

"We'll use this wood to help us swim," says Jake.

"Yay-hey, that's the way!" says Izzy.

"The river looks like a rainbow flowing down the waterfall," says Smee.

"Did you say . . . waterfall?"
asks Hook.
Hook and Smee cannot stop.
"Lose the surfy-thing!" yells Hook.

Can you name
all the colors in
Rainbow River?

Hook and Smee jump off the surfboard.
They grab on to a vine.

"Are you okay?" asks Jake.

"We are fine. Move along," says Hook.

"Oh, no! The surfboard is heading toward the waterfall," says Izzy.

"Crackers," says Skully.
"We'll never see the surfboard again!"
"Yes, we will," says Jake.

"I'll lend a helping fin,"
says Marina.
They race toward the surfboard.
"Full speed ahead!" says Jake.

"Be careful, Jake," says Marina.
Jake jumps onto the surfboard.

It is too late!
"Wipeout!" yells Marina.
"We're going over the waterfall!"

"If only the surfboard could fly,"
says Marina.

"It can!" says Jake.

Izzy sprinkles the surfboard
with Pixie Dust.
"Wheee!" calls Marina.

What does Izzy use to make the surfboard fly?

The flying surfboard soars over
Rainbow River.
"Need a ride?" asks Jake.
"Oh yes, thank you," says Smee.

"I don't take rides from puny pirates or flying fish!" says Hook. "Whatever you say, Captain," says Izzy.

"Surf's up!" calls Cubby.
"Let's hit the waves,"
says Izzy.

Jake and his crew have an awesome time!

What do you see on the crew's surfboards?

"We can't hang around all day,"
says Smee.

THUMP! Hook jumps onto a log.

"I'm surfing, Smee!"

Just then, they hear . . .
Tick-tock! Tick-tock!
"That's not a log," says Smee.
"It's the Croc!"

How many logs are
in the river?

"What are you waiting for?"
calls Hook.
"Save me, Smee!"

"Right away. Here I come, Cap'n!"
says Smee.

"For solving pirate problems today, we earned ten Gold Doubloons!" says Jake.
"Well done, crew," says Izzy.

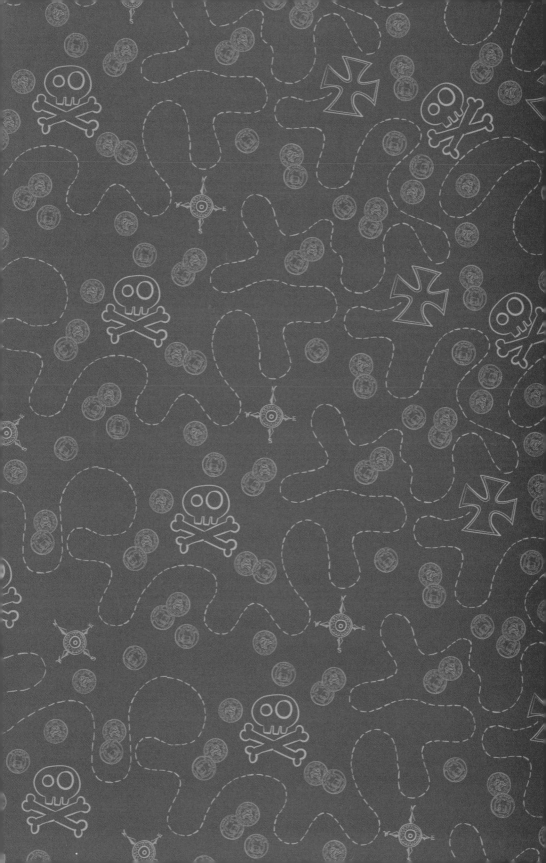